THIS WALKER BOOK BELONGS TO:

_____

_____

_____

For Wendy and Matthew

First published 1991 by Walker Books Ltd
87 Vauxhall Walk, London SE11 5HJ

This edition published 2006

15 14 13 12

© 1991, 2006 Marcia Williams

The right of Marcia Williams to be identified as author/
illustrator of this work has been asserted by her in accordance
with the Copyright, Designs and Patents Act 1988

This book has been typeset in Goudy

Printed in China

British Library Cataloguing in Publication Data:
a catalogue record for this book is
available from the British Library

ISBN 978-1-4063-0347-6

www.walker.co.uk

GREEK MYTHS

❖❖ RETOLD AND ILLUSTRATED BY ❖❖
MARCIA WILLIAMS

WALKER BOOKS
AND SUBSIDIARIES
LONDON · BOSTON · SYDNEY · AUCKLAND

PANDORA'S BOX

Aren't we a heavenly lot, Zeus?

In the beginning, the gods lived on Mount Olympus.

But only giants and wild beasts lived on earth.

My little dolls.

Then the giant Prometheus made people out of clay

Can you puff a bit of life into this lot?

and Zeus breathed life into them.

Prometheus taught mankind all he knew,

Best to keep on their right side by making the odd sacrifice.

including respect for the gods.

What have we done wrong? Ho! Ho! Ho! I sacrificed two hens and a cow last week! Maybe he's a vegetarian.

Zeus occasionally sent a thunderbolt hurtling to earth to remind mankind of his power,

Just so long as you do as you're told.

but otherwise, harmony reigned ...

Very droll, but I like my fun to be a bit spicier.

until Prometheus played a trick on Zeus.

Am I getting a whiff of spice here?

Confused as to how to offer a sacrificial bull to Zeus, some men asked Prometheus to show them what to do.

PRIME GREEK RUMP

He put a steak on top of one sack of guts and eyeballs.

Then he put guts on top of a sack of chops and steak.

Prometheus then offered both sacks to Zeus.

Zeus chose the one with steak on top,

but when he discovered the true contents, he roared with anger.

In revenge, Zeus extinguished every spark of fire on earth,

leaving mankind cold and hungry.

But Prometheus did not wish his beloved humans to suffer.

So he stole up Mount Olympus, and broke off a blazing piece of sun for the people.

For this, Zeus punished Prometheus by chaining him to a rock.

Each day a great vulture tore out his liver. And each night, his liver grew again. The torture continued for months before Prometheus was released.

Zeus also punished mankind. He ordered the gods to create a beautiful woman.

Her name was Pandora and she was to be married to Prometheus' brother.

Epimetheus, fearful of Zeus, married Pandora at once.

Pandora was vain and self-centred.

She nagged her husband constantly.

She demanded he open a special locked box. Epimetheus refused,

as Prometheus had entrusted the box to his care.

In that box was trapped every known evil and disease.

But her husband's stubbornness made Pandora more determined.

Convinced the box held jewels, she planned to steal it.

One day, while Epimetheus slept,

Pandora stole the box and its key.

Eagerly, she fitted the key into the lock.

It turned, and she lifted the lid...

All at once, every evil and spite flew out, like a swarm of insects,
covering Pandora and infesting the earth with pain and sorrow.

Luckily, Prometheus had also locked "hope" in the box,
so mankind was saved from total despair. But – thanks
to Pandora – life on earth was never quite so joyful again.

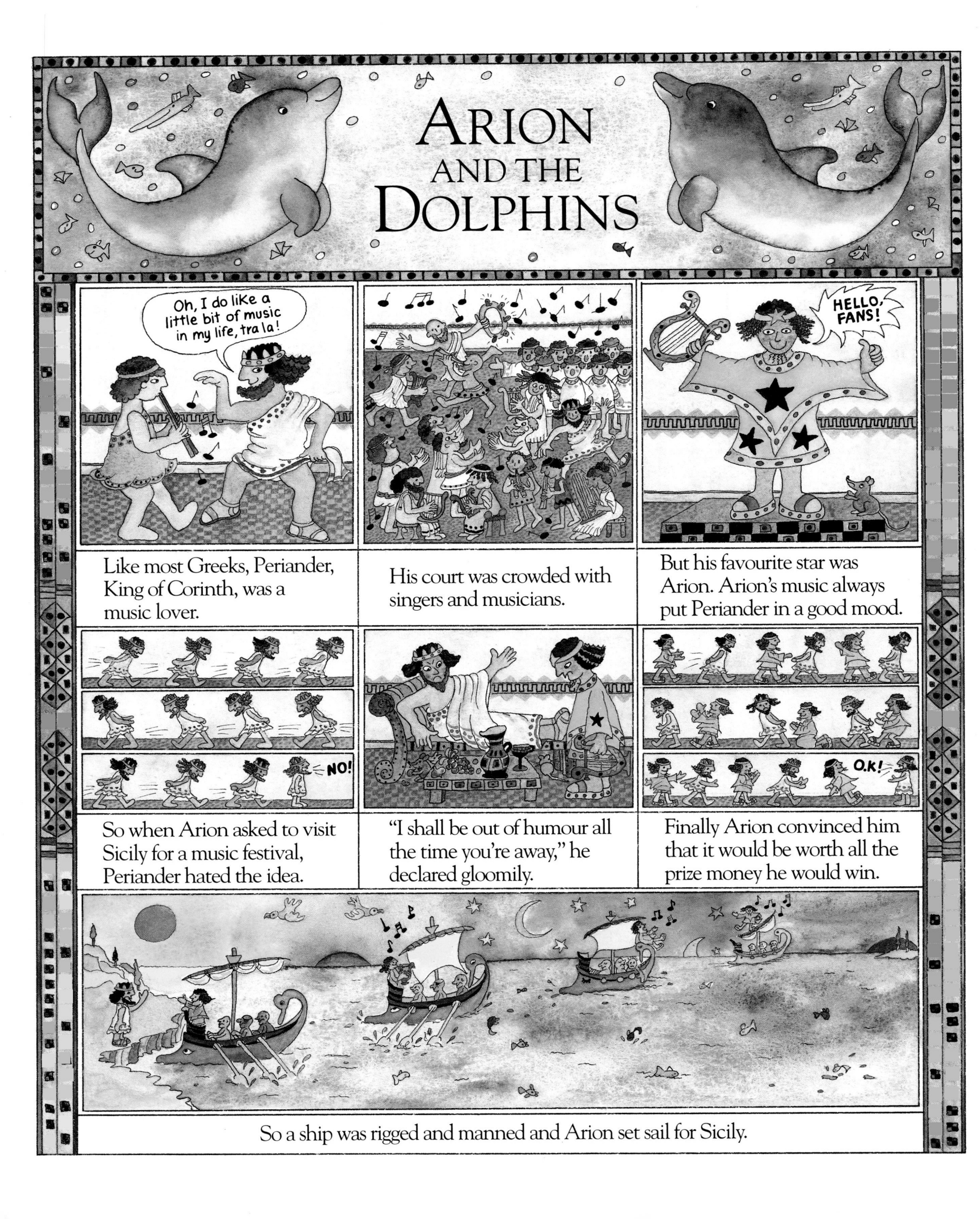

ARION AND THE DOLPHINS

Like most Greeks, Periander, King of Corinth, was a music lover.

His court was crowded with singers and musicians.

But his favourite star was Arion. Arion's music always put Periander in a good mood.

So when Arion asked to visit Sicily for a music festival, Periander hated the idea.

"I shall be out of humour all the time you're away," he declared gloomily.

Finally Arion convinced him that it would be worth all the prize money he would win.

So a ship was rigged and manned and Arion set sail for Sicily.

Once there, it seemed that Arion could not play or sing a wrong note.

He won so many prizes that it took twelve porters to carry them to the ship.

Arion was delighted to be returning home to Periander with such fame and fortune.

The sailors were delighted too, for they had a mind to steal the prizes.

When the ship was well out to sea, they surrounded Arion with shouts of, "You must die!"

Arion tried to persuade them to take his gold and spare his life.

But the sailors felt they would only be safe with Arion dead.

Arion pleaded to be allowed to sing one last song.

He knelt on the prow and sang to the gods to look on him kindly.

Then, as the last notes died away, he threw himself into the sea.

The waves closed over him and the ship sailed on.

Periander was all for having the murderous thieves executed on the spot,

but Arion was more merciful and begged that they be allowed to live.

So Periander banished them to an ugly, barbarous land.

This done, Periander settled back to enjoy some of Arion's finest singing.

As the music floated around him, Periander's thoughts grew calm and, for the first time since Arion's departure, a smile came to his lips.

Orpheus and Eurydice

Orpheus was a famous poet and musician. People came from all over Greece to hear him play his lyre and sing.

His music made wild beasts tame, and trees bend to listen.

Orpheus loved the beautiful nymph, Eurydice. The day they married was the happiest in his life.

Eurydice loved dancing and often went to romp in the fields. But one day, dancing among the meadow flowers, she trod upon a deadly snake.

The snake sank its poisonous fangs into her ankle. Eurydice, overcome by the fatal poison, died instantly.

Orpheus, when he heard the news, was inconsolable and for days would neither eat nor drink. His friends feared for his life.

Then, without a word, he took his lyre and left the house. He travelled to Hades, the land of the dead, to beg for the return of his beloved Eurydice.

At last he came to the River Styx, on the edge of the underworld, where Charon, the ferryman, waited to carry the dead across.

At first Charon refused to take the living Orpheus.

But when Orpheus played to him upon his lyre, Charon relented.

On the other side of the river, Orpheus' journey became a nightmare.

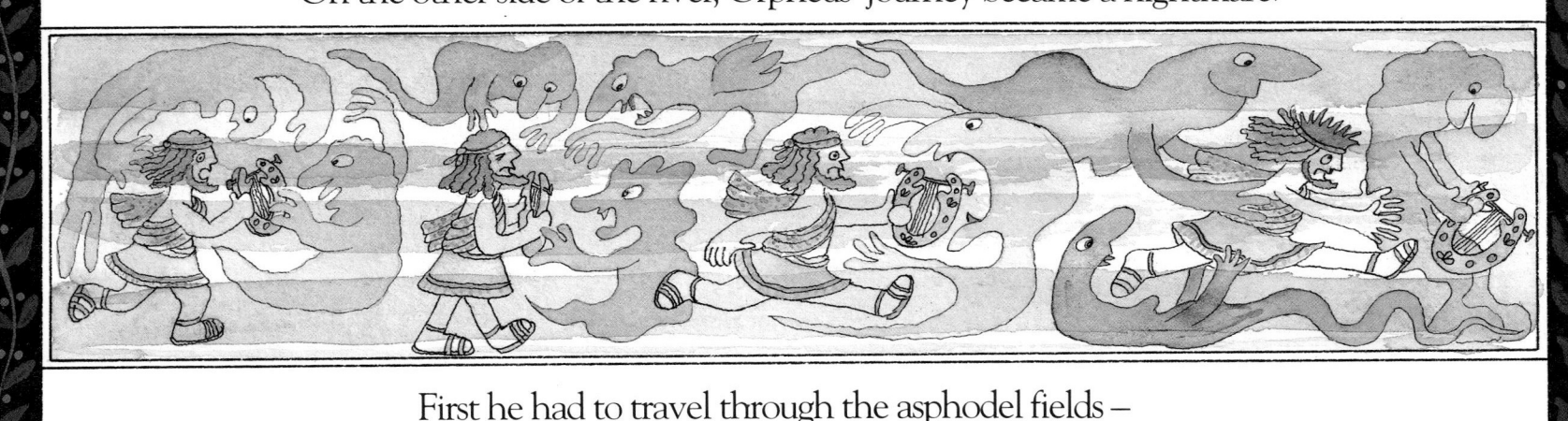

First he had to travel through the asphodel fields –
fields that were dark and grey and haunted by ghosts.

Then on he went through Tartarus, where the evil were tortured and
where the guard-dog, Cerberus, growled and snapped at his heels.

Finally, Orpheus reached the centre. He knelt before King Pluto and his queen, Persephone,
who were amazed that a living person should risk his life to reach their kingdom.

Orpheus then took up his lyre and sang of his love for Eurydice
and of his great sorrow. Pluto and Persephone were moved to tears.

They agreed to release Eurydice, on one condition:

Orpheus was not to look back until he reached the world of the living.
So Orpheus departed, without knowing whether Eurydice followed or not.

As he came to the River Styx, he hesitated: if Pluto and Persephone
had tricked him, this was his last chance to go back.

With one foot in the boat, Orpheus turned –
and saw his beloved Eurydice, smiling upon him.

But then her living form faded and Eurydice
became a ghost of the underworld.

And as Charon slowly ferried him into the sunlit world, Orpheus
realized that this time he had lost his love for ever.

THE TWELVE TASKS OF HERACLES

Heracles was a tough little baby.

Everyone loved him but Hera, Zeus' wife, who sent two snakes to kill him.

But Heracles strangled both of them.

For a while, Hera ignored Heracles.

As he grew up, Heracles became stronger and stronger and stronger.

He married and had many children.

Hera hated him being so happy.

So one night she put a spell on him. He lashed out with his sword, killing imaginary enemies.

But when he woke, he saw he had killed his own children.

Heart-broken, Heracles went to the temple to seek forgiveness.

The priestess said he could make amends by serving his old enemy, King Eurystheus.

The King was frightened of Heracles, so he hid in a pot whenever he came near.

And because he hated Heracles, he gave him twelve deadly tasks.

First, Heracles had to kill a huge lion whose hide was so thick that no sword could penetrate it.

Next, he had to kill the many-headed Hydra, whose very breath could kill man or beast.

Thirdly, he had to capture the sacred, golden-horned deer, an animal as quick as the wind.

The fourth task was to catch a savage boar whose tusks could pierce any armour.

Next, Heracles had to clean out, in one night, the vast and filthy stables of King Augeas.

The eleventh, to collect three golden apples protected by a ferocious dragon.

Heracles' twelfth and last task was the most dangerous of all: to fetch the three-headed guard dog, Cerberus, from Hell itself.

His twelve tasks completed, Heracles returned to King Eurystheus.

The King was dismayed to see him alive, and quickly sent him packing.

Then, to avoid angering the gods, Heracles sent Cerberus back to Hades.

At the temple, Heracles was finally pardoned.

He was content at last, and stronger than ever!

And Hera never bothered Heracles again.

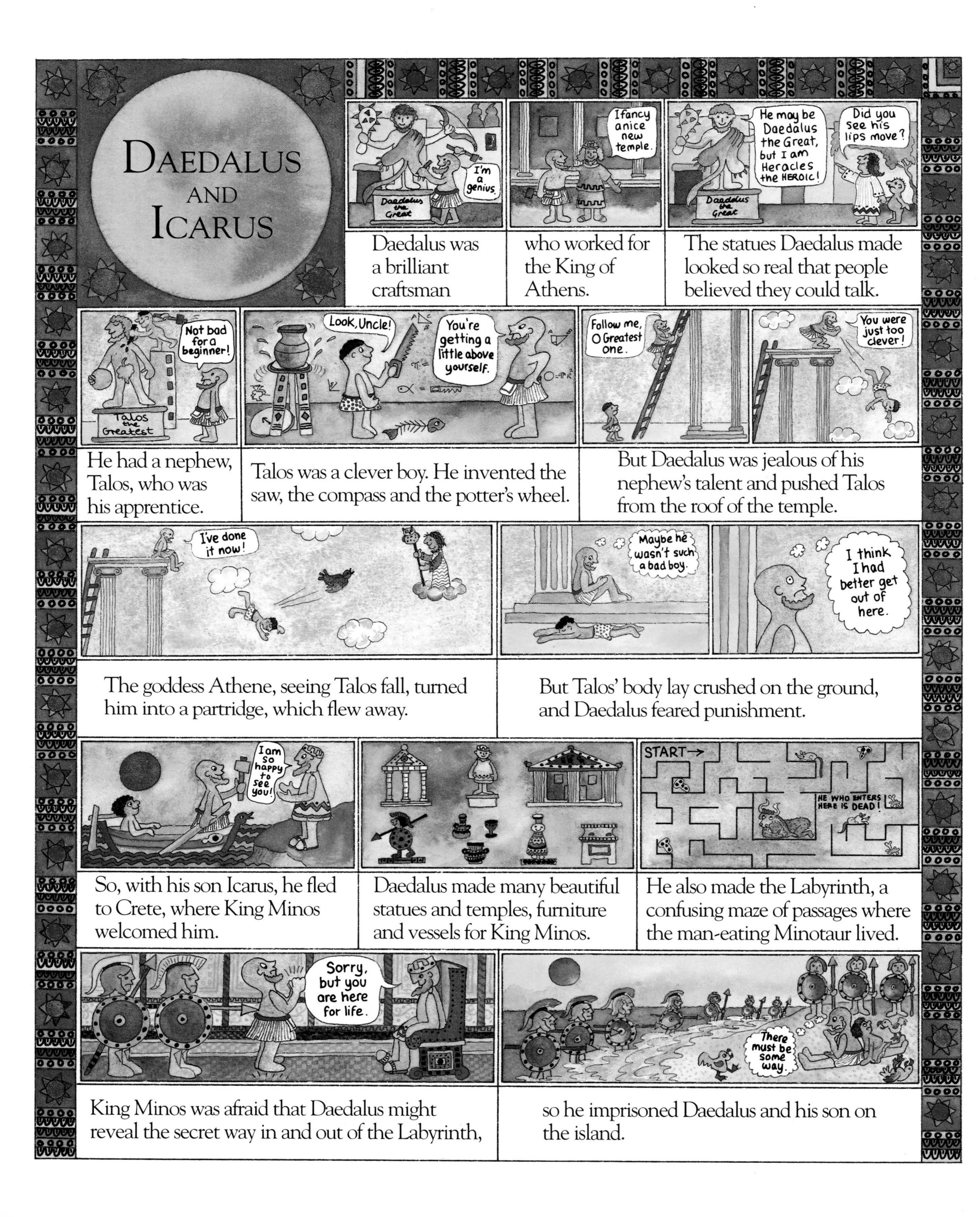

DAEDALUS AND ICARUS

Daedalus was a brilliant craftsman

who worked for the King of Athens.

The statues Daedalus made looked so real that people believed they could talk.

He had a nephew, Talos, who was his apprentice.

Talos was a clever boy. He invented the saw, the compass and the potter's wheel.

But Daedalus was jealous of his nephew's talent and pushed Talos from the roof of the temple.

The goddess Athene, seeing Talos fall, turned him into a partridge, which flew away.

But Talos' body lay crushed on the ground, and Daedalus feared punishment.

So, with his son Icarus, he fled to Crete, where King Minos welcomed him.

Daedalus made many beautiful statues and temples, furniture and vessels for King Minos.

He also made the Labyrinth, a confusing maze of passages where the man-eating Minotaur lived.

King Minos was afraid that Daedalus might reveal the secret way in and out of the Labyrinth,

so he imprisoned Daedalus and his son on the island.

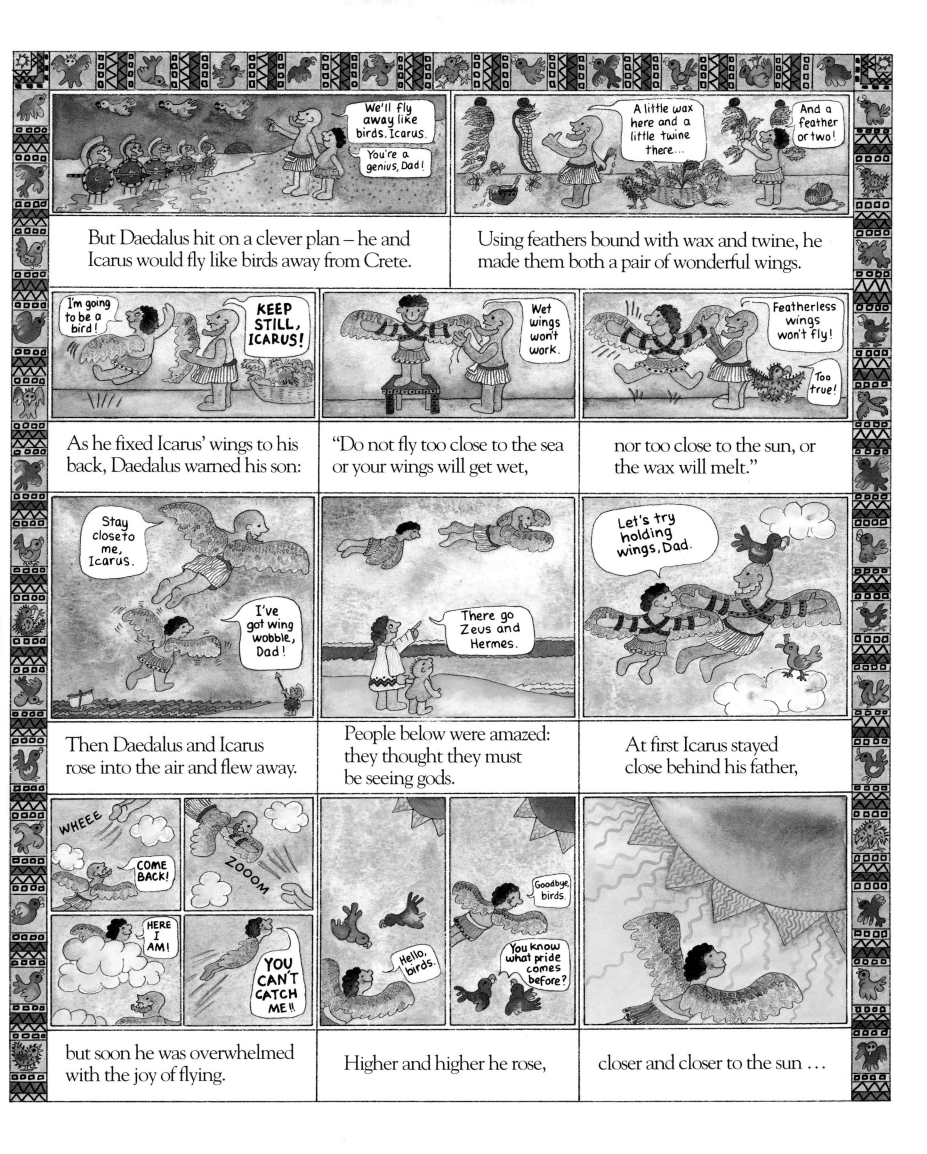

But Daedalus hit on a clever plan – he and Icarus would fly like birds away from Crete.

Using feathers bound with wax and twine, he made them both a pair of wonderful wings.

As he fixed Icarus' wings to his back, Daedalus warned his son:

"Do not fly too close to the sea or your wings will get wet,

nor too close to the sun, or the wax will melt."

Then Daedalus and Icarus rose into the air and flew away.

People below were amazed: they thought they must be seeing gods.

At first Icarus stayed close behind his father,

but soon he was overwhelmed with the joy of flying.

Higher and higher he rose,

closer and closer to the sun …

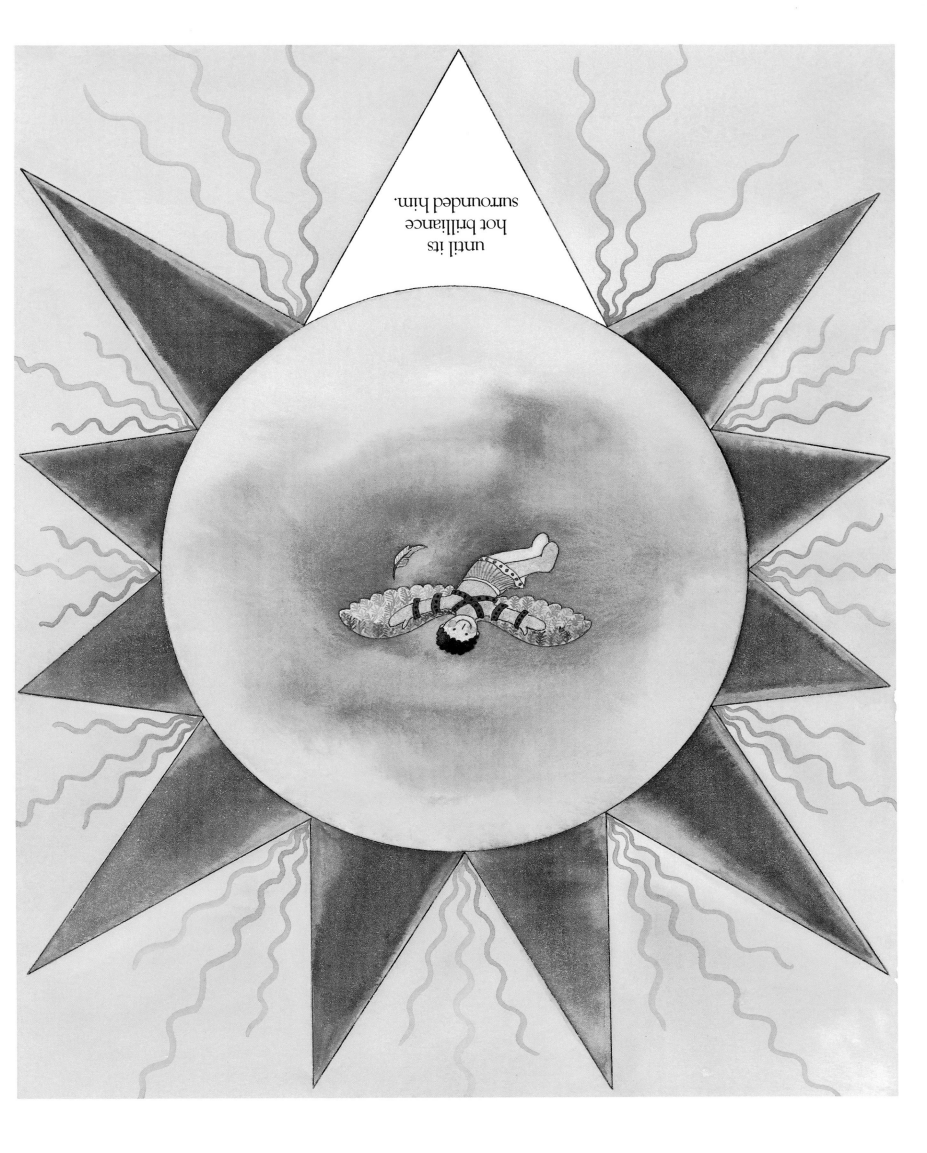

until its
hot brilliance
surrounded him.

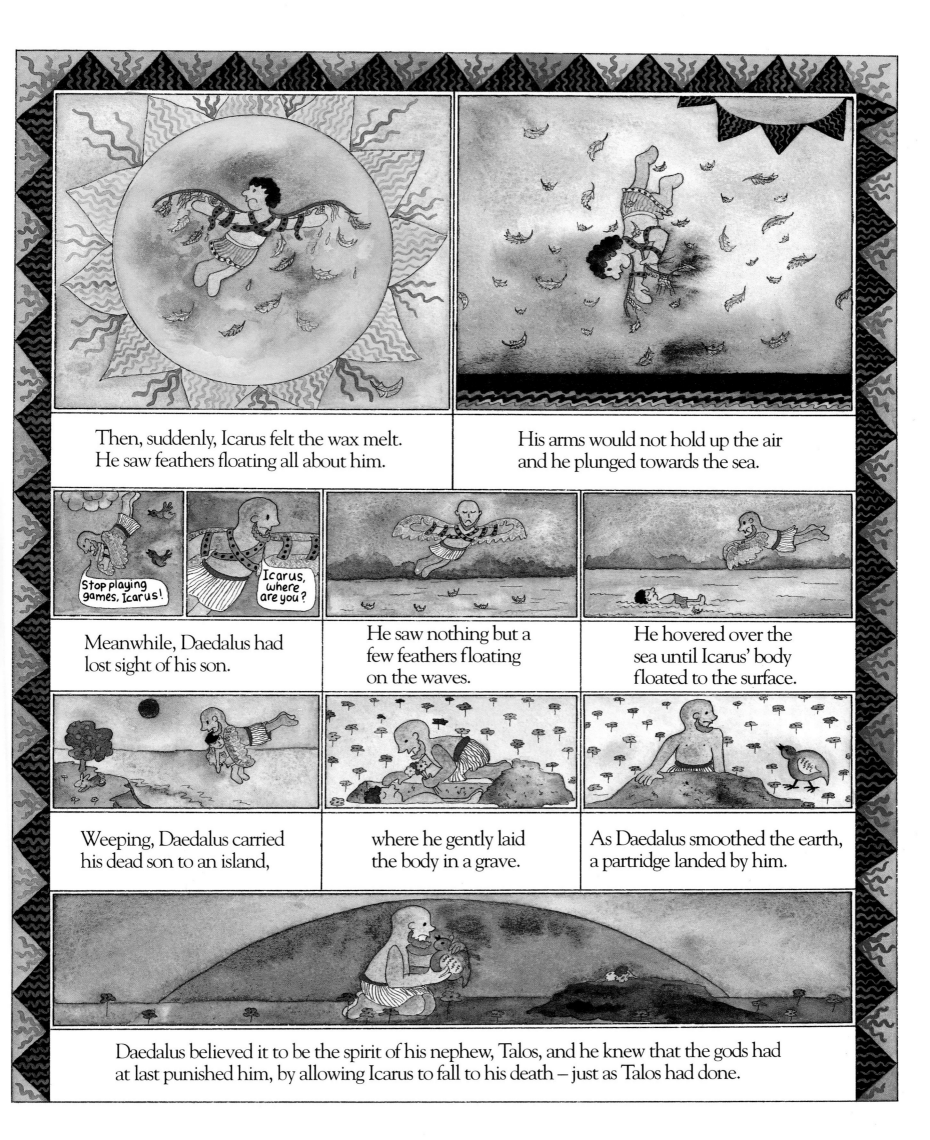

Then, suddenly, Icarus felt the wax melt. He saw feathers floating all about him.

His arms would not hold up the air and he plunged towards the sea.

Meanwhile, Daedalus had lost sight of his son.

He saw nothing but a few feathers floating on the waves.

He hovered over the sea until Icarus' body floated to the surface.

Weeping, Daedalus carried his dead son to an island,

where he gently laid the body in a grave.

As Daedalus smoothed the earth, a partridge landed by him.

Daedalus believed it to be the spirit of his nephew, Talos, and he knew that the gods had at last punished him, by allowing Icarus to fall to his death – just as Talos had done.

PERSEUS
AND THE GORGON'S HEAD

King Acrisius of Argos was a worried man.

He had been warned that his daughter, Danaë, would have a son who would kill him.

So when Danaë bore a baby boy, named Perseus,

Acrisius put them both in a wooden chest

and pushed the vessel out to sea.

For days the chest tossed on the waves.

Finally, it washed up on the shores of Seriphos

where Dictys, the brother of King Polydectes, found it.

He was amazed to see Danaë and Perseus inside.

The grumpy King allowed them to stay in the palace.

Perseus grew up strong and handsome.

Meanwhile, the King fell in love with Danaë.

He proposed to her at every opportunity.

And at every opportunity, Danaë refused him.

Polydectes plotted to get rid of Perseus by sending him on a deadly mission.

Still Danaë refused to marry the King.

So Polydectes sent Perseus to fetch the head of the Gorgon, Medusa.

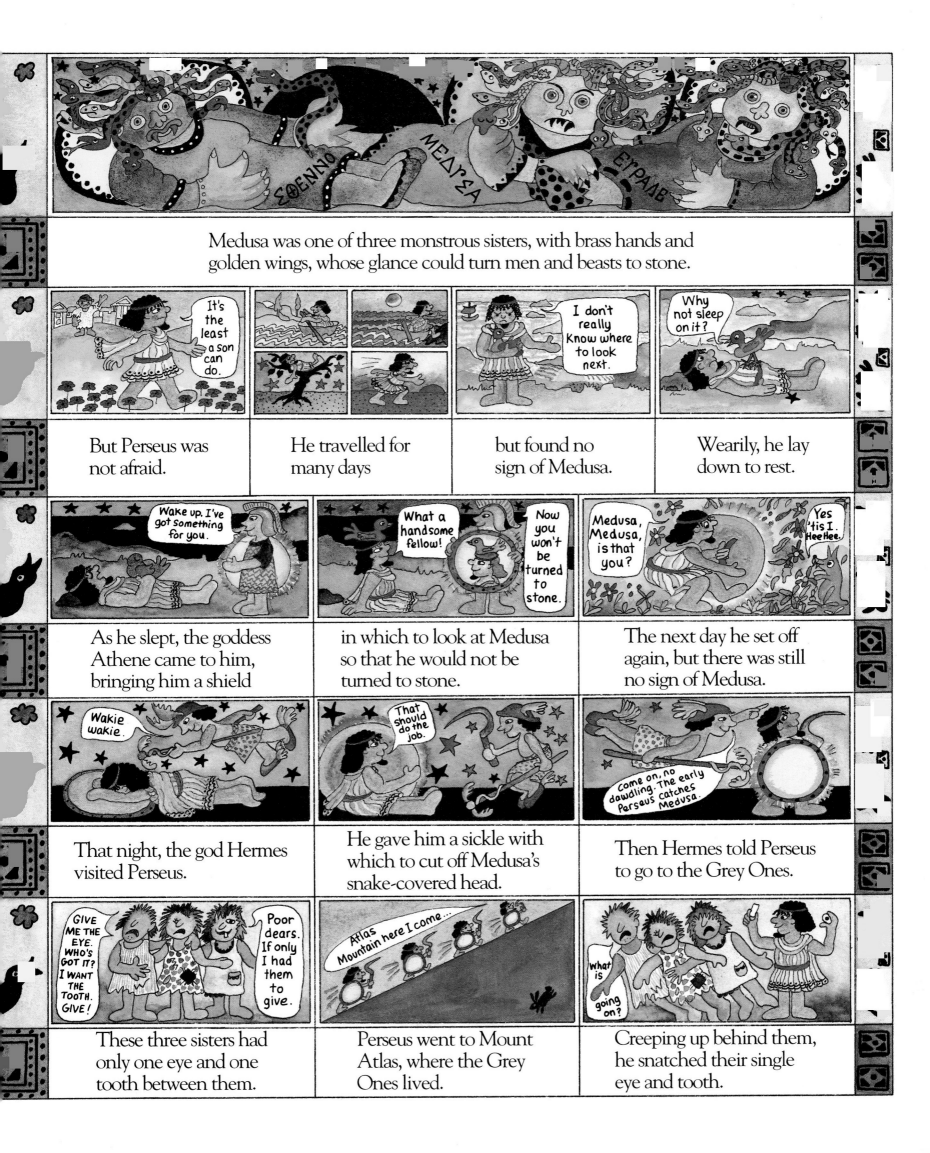

Medusa was one of three monstrous sisters, with brass hands and golden wings, whose glance could turn men and beasts to stone.

But Perseus was not afraid.

He travelled for many days

but found no sign of Medusa.

Wearily, he lay down to rest.

As he slept, the goddess Athene came to him, bringing him a shield

in which to look at Medusa so that he would not be turned to stone.

The next day he set off again, but there was still no sign of Medusa.

That night, the god Hermes visited Perseus.

He gave him a sickle with which to cut off Medusa's snake-covered head.

Then Hermes told Perseus to go to the Grey Ones.

These three sisters had only one eye and one tooth between them.

Perseus went to Mount Atlas, where the Grey Ones lived.

Creeping up behind them, he snatched their single eye and tooth.

So they told him he must
seek out the Ocean Nymphs.

and Perseus agreed, in
exchange for information.

The Grey Ones screamed
for them to be returned

They hated Medusa and were
glad to assist Perseus.

Upon reaching the ocean,
he called to the Nymphs.

Then Perseus returned the
eye and tooth and went on.

and a bag in which to put
Medusa's deadly head.

a helmet to make him
completely invisible,

They gave him winged
sandals, so he could fly,

Looking into his shield,
he beheld a fearful sight.

There, Perseus heard their
rumbling, growling snores.

Then they directed him to
where the Gorgons lived.

In a moment, he had it
in the bag.

and with one mighty stroke,
sliced off Medusa's head.

Fearlessly, Perseus raised
his sickle high...

Great storms battered the little ship on its journey to Crete.

When Theseus finally landed, he found King Minos waiting, with his daughter Ariadne.

Ariadne immediately fell madly in love with Theseus,

and she resolved to save him from the Minotaur and marry him.

That night, Ariadne crept softly past the guards.

She gave Theseus a sword, and a ball of magic thread to guide him out of the maze.

Next day, the Athenians were thrown into the Labyrinth.

Once inside, Theseus tied one end of the thread to the door and set off in search of the Minotaur.

Some led nowhere.

Others took him deeper into the maze.

The roar of the Minotaur grew louder.

ROAR!

The struggle was long and fierce, for the Minotaur was enormously strong.

But Theseus eventually drove his sword through its heart and it sank to the ground – dead.

Following the thread, Theseus traced his path back to the entrance of the Labyrinth.

Hearing the cheers of Theseus' friends, Ariadne quickly unlocked the door.

Then everyone ran for the ship and set sail for Athens.

After a few days, they stopped at an island, where Ariadne fell asleep.

Theseus, unwilling to marry his enemy's daughter, left her sleeping on the sand.

In all this excitement, Theseus forgot to change his sail from black to white.

Meanwhile, his father, King Aegeus, watched anxiously for his ship.

Sighting the black sail, and thinking the worst, he cast himself on to the rocks below.

As Athenian parents celebrated their children's return, Theseus mourned the death of his father.

So the sad, but heroic Theseus became King of Athens and lived to win many more victories.

ARACHNE VERSUS **ATHENE**

Arachne lived with her father in a poor Greek village.

She was not a very beautiful girl, or a very nice one.

But she was brilliant at weaving, probably better than anyone else in Greece.

Arachne certainly thought so, and never tired of telling others.

Many people thought that her skill must have been learned from the great goddess, Athene.

But the arrogant Arachne denied this, believing that she was even cleverer than the goddess.

This boasting was unwise, for the gods were quick to anger, when humans claimed great powers.

Morning, noon and night, Arachne's father begged her not to compare herself to Athene.

But nothing checked Arachne's conceited tongue. She even challenged Athene to a weaving contest.

Soon afterwards, an ugly old woman came to Arachne.

She told Arachne to withdraw her challenge to Athene.

Arachne laughed, declaring that she could out-weave anyone.

The old woman quivered from head to toe with rage, until suddenly …

she was transformed into her true self – the all-powerful goddess, Athene.

Even then the foolish Arachne was unafraid. Athene decided, therefore, to teach her a lesson.

So two looms were set side by side and the amazing contest began.

All day the shuttles flashed back and forth, weaving designs in marvellous colours.

Athene's cloth depicted the gods in all their glory.

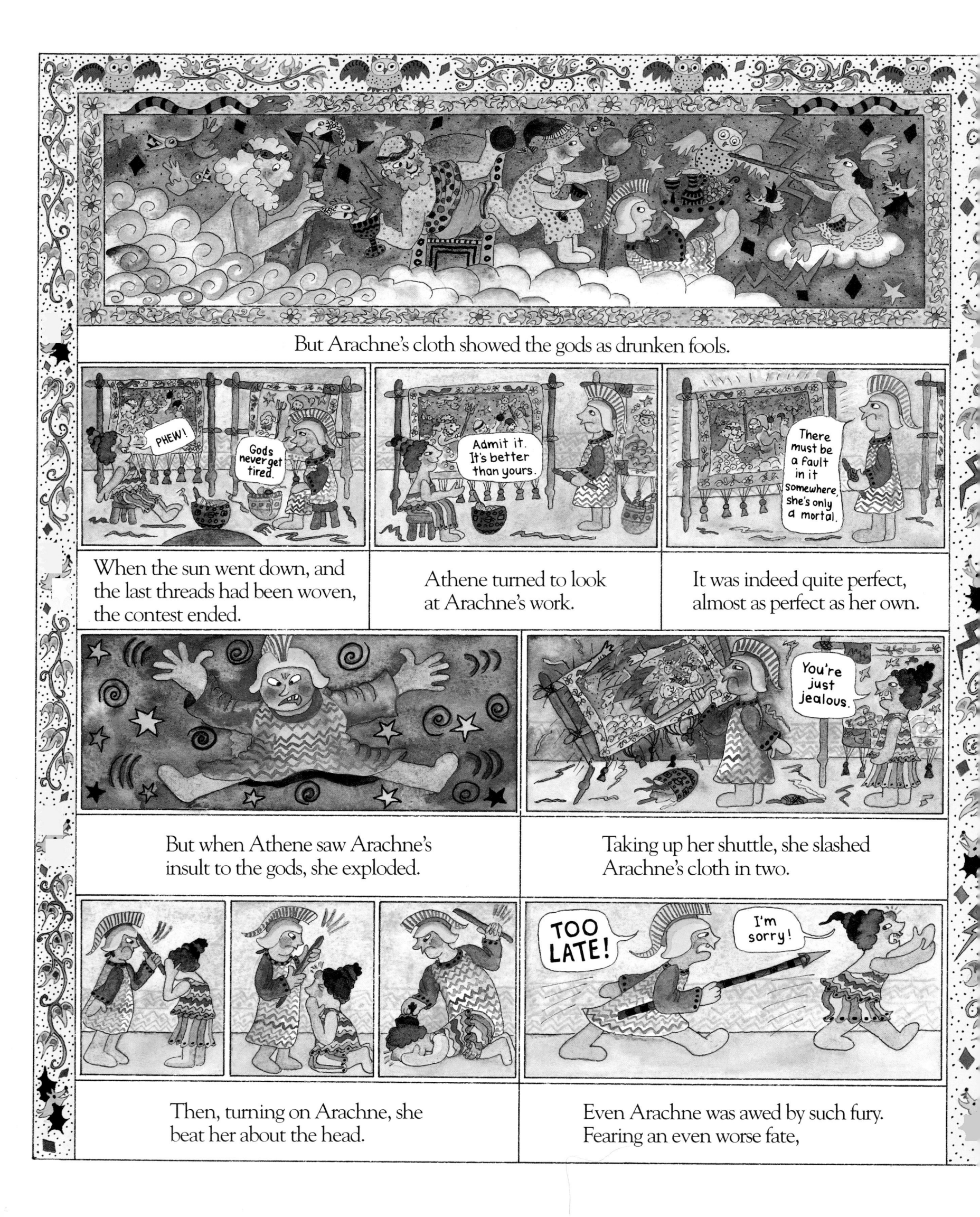

But Arachne's cloth showed the gods as drunken fools.

When the sun went down, and the last threads had been woven, the contest ended.

Athene turned to look at Arachne's work.

It was indeed quite perfect, almost as perfect as her own.

But when Athene saw Arachne's insult to the gods, she exploded.

Taking up her shuttle, she slashed Arachne's cloth in two.

Then, turning on Arachne, she beat her about the head.

Even Arachne was awed by such fury. Fearing an even worse fate, she tied a noose round her neck and hanged herself from a beam.

There she swayed, the life slowly being squeezed out of her body.

Arachne's father, horrified at her plight, begged Athene to spare his daughter.

Grudgingly, the goddess agreed to let her rival live.

She sprinkled herbs upon Arachne – and there began a dreadful transformation.

First, Arachne's hair fell out.

Then her nose, ears and legs fell off.

Her arms disappeared, so that her fingers cleaved to her sides.

Her head and body shrank, until she was no bigger than a fist.

And finally, the rope by which Arachne dangled became a fine, silken thread.

Athene had taken her revenge – she had turned the boastful Arachne into a spider!

Marcia Williams

With her distinctive cartoon-strip style, lively text and brilliant wit, Marcia Williams brings
to life some of the world's all-time favourite stories and some colourful historical characters.
Her hilarious retellings and clever observations will have children
laughing out loud and coming back for more!

ISBN 978-1-4063-3523-1

ISBN 978-1-4063-3832-4

ISBN 978-1-4063-2997-1

ISBN 978-1-4063-0563-0

ISBN 978-1-4063-2334-4

ISBN 978-1-4063-2335-1

ISBN 978-1-4063-2610-9

ISBN 978-1-4063-1944-6

ISBN 978-1-4063-1866-1

ISBN 978-1-4063-0562-3

ISBN 978-1-4063-0348-3

ISBN 978-1-4063-0347-6

ISBN 978-1-4063-0171-7

ISBN 978-1-4063-0940-9

ISBN 978-1-4063-1002-3

Available from all good booksellers

www.walker.co.uk